KT-222-251

THIS WALKER BOOK BELONGS TO:

BRISTOL CITY LIBRARIES
WITHDRAWN AND OFFERED FOR SALE

First published 2011 by Walker Books Ltd
87 Vauxhall Walk, London SE11 5HJ

This edition published 2012

6 8 10 9 7

© 2011 Brun Limited

The right of Anthony Browne to be identified as author/illustrator of this work has been
asserted by him in accordance with the Copyright, Designs and Patents Act 1988

This book has been typeset in Gill Sans

Printed in China

All rights reserved. No part of this book may be reproduced, transmitted or stored in
an information retrieval system in any form or by any means, graphic, electronic or
mechanical, including photocopying, taping and recording, without prior written
permission from the publisher.

British Library Cataloguing in Publication Data:
a catalogue record for this book is available from the British Library

ISBN 978-1-4063-3851-5

www.walker.co.uk

How Do
YOU
Feel?

Anthony Browne

WALKER BOOKS
AND SUBSIDIARIES
LONDON • BOSTON • SYDNEY • AUCKLAND

How do you feel?

Well, sometimes I feel **bored** …

and sometimes I feel

lonely.

Sometimes I feel very happy ...

and sometimes I feel *sad*.

I feel ANGRY ...

and sometimes I feel **guilty**.

Sometimes I feel curious ...

but then sometimes I'm **SURPRISED!**

I feel **CONFIDENT** ...

but I can also feel *shy*.

I can feel a bit worried ...

but more often I feel REALLY SILLY!

Sometimes I feel very hungry ...

and sometimes very **FULL**.

Right now, I feel a little sleepy.

How do
YOU
feel?

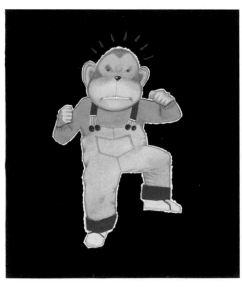

Anthony Browne

Acclaimed Children's Laureate from 2009 to 2011 and winner of multiple awards – including the prestigious Kate Greenaway Medal and the much coveted Hans Christian Andersen Award – Anthony is one of the most celebrated author–illustrators of his generation. Renowned for his unique style, his work is recognized and loved throughout the world.

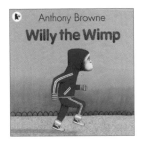

Willy the Wimp
ISBN 978-1-4063-1874-6

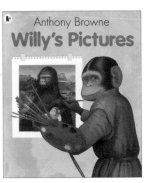

Willy's Pictures
ISBN 978-1-4063-1356-7

Willy the Dreamer
ISBN 978-1-4063-1357-4

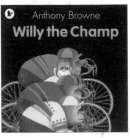

Willy the Champ
ISBN 978-1-4063-1873-9

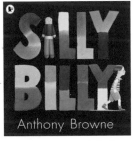

Silly Billy
ISBN 978-1-4063-0576-0

Things I Like
ISBN 978-0-7445-9858-2

Hansel and Gretel
ISBN 978-1-4063-1852-4

I Like Books
ISBN 978-0-7445-9857-5

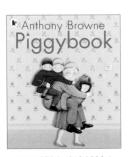

Piggybook
ISBN 978-1-4063-1328-4

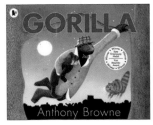

Gorilla
ISBN 978-1-4063-1327-7

Little Beauty
ISBN 978-1-4063-1930-9

Changes
ISBN 978-1-4063-1339-0

The Tunnel
ISBN 978-1-4063-1329-1

Available from all good booksellers

www.walker.co.uk